The Power of a Friend

The Power of A Friend

Written By
Sade R Harvison

Xulon Press
2301 Lucien Way #415
Maitland, FL 32751
407.339.4217
www.xulonpress.com

Library of Congress Control Number: 2021-911574

Paperback ISBN-13: 978-1-66282-013-7
Hardcover ISBN-13: 978-1-66282-014-4
Ebook ISBN-13: 978-1-66282-015-1

I would like to dedicate this book to all the little lotus flowers in the world. Just remember you were made to blossom through the darkness and the mud.

Special Acknowledgement

I would like to acknowledge one of my best childhood friends. Her name is Krystal Collins. We met cheering, but turns out we shared a common pain. Through this pain a sweet childhood friendship flourished. I just want her to know that our friendship made my childhood just a little sweeter. I hope I was able to do the same for her.

There was a little girl
named Lo'Tuz
who was surrounded
by love.

She had a smile that was
as bright as the sun.

LO'TUZ was so beautiful and bright,

but she would cry herself to sleep late at night.

See, Lo'Tuz wasn't like most boys and girls.

Her mommy was some-
where lost in the world.

9

Then one day, at cheer practice, along came a special friend.

Together they would begin
to help each other's hearts mend.

11

She, too, had a mommy
who sometimes went away.

But that didn't seem to matter when the two of them would play.

They would cheer, they would dance,
and they'd talk about their moms.

This was the start of a childhood bond.

You may feel sad—
you might even feel blue.

But remember: there could be
a special friend made just for you.

About the author

Sade R. Harvison was born in Columbus, Ohio on November 16, 1988 to Victor Harvison and Catrinna Brock. Sade would describe her younger years as a time filled with love and chaos. This inspired her to write a childrens book series based on her time growing up in Columbus, Ohio to young parents in the '90s. She really wanted to paint a picture and describe how she was able to navigate life without being raised by her mother. Sade hopes that the Lo'Tuz series will help young children who struggle with similar situations. She wants them to know through her own life story, that some of the most beautiful things come alive in the dark. Most importantly she wants to show her three sons that with vision and dedication nothing can stop you!

CPSIA information can be obtained
at www.ICGtesting.com
Printed in the USA
BVRC101732110721
611675BV00004B/6